MY RACIST GRAN: SAYS WE STILL CAN'T TRUST THE JAPS

I have over 100 humor books and several strange coloring books available on Amazon.

My humor books cover a wide range of topics and styles, from dumb jokes and puns to satirical takes on current events. Whatever your sense of humor, you'll find something to love or hate in my collection.

And for those who want to tap into their creative side, my strange coloring books offer unique and unconventional designs for you to color in and make your own. These books are perfect for relaxing after a long day, or for getting in touch with your inner artist.

So don't wait any longer to add some laughter and creativity to your life. Check out my other books on Amazon today!

Here are just a few...

books.bradgosse.com

THE HOLIDAYS ARE WHEN WE GO

TO GRANDMAS HOUSE RIGHT THROUGH THE SNOW

WE LOVE HER TURKEY CANNOT LIE

UNTIL GRAN GETS THAT LOOK IN HER EYE

ONE DRINK – TWO DRINK – THREE DRINK – FOUR

GRANDMA SUDDENLY REMEMBERS THE WAR

REMEMBER WHY TO KEEP A STRAIGHT FACE

WHEN LIGHT DINNER CONVERSATION TURNS TO RACE

EVEN WHILE THE GIFTS UNWRAP

GRANDMA WON'T SHUT UP ABOUT THE JAPS

BLACK PEOPLE – BROWN PEOPLE – POLISH OR JEW

OUR GRANDMOTHER PROBABLY HATES YOU

ON THE DRIVE HOME OUR DADDY WILL SAY

"REMEMBER WE DIDN'T BRING YOU UP THAT WAY"

DAD CLAIMS TO BE THE GREAT DEFENDER

UNTIL THE CONVERSATION, TURNS TO GENDER

MIKE HUNT SMELLS LIKE FISH

Clap along with Mike Hunt. This book is filled with hilarious double entendres. You know what it's about. Don't make me spell it out for you. This book is cheap as balls. Like your mom.

MIKE LIT
Shouldn't Be Hard To Find

Every girl, and some guys want my big black hawk. This book teaches you why big black hawks matter.

ALL THE GIRLS LOVE MY BIG BLACK HAWK

CUCUMBER CURTIS

Can't come to dinner. Your mom has other plans for this innocent little vegetable.

GLUCK GLUCK 3000

Sex Robots are the new wave of the future in sexual entertainment. In fact, they're already in the process of being built. Catering to the needs of lonely men and women, these bots will soon be ubiquitous.

SEXTOY STORY

RACE WARS

Black, car, white car, and yellow car too.

STD'S & YOU

Learning From The Animals At The Zoo

BAA BAA BLACK SHEEP
Deals With Another Routine Stop

Baa baa black sheep please step out of the car. Yes sir yes sir please know I'm unarmed. Do you know why I stopped you today?. "Because of the fur color I display?". You match the description of a suspect I seek. Funny it's the 4th time to happen this week. I profiled you because you are black. And you drive a Mercedes which seems kinda whack.

CLIP CLOP
The Racist Horse Cop

Does Anyone Know Whatever Happened To MURDER HORNETS

Remember Murder Hornets? Whatever happened to them? We dive deeply into the terror phenomenon that never came to be. 2020 had so many bigger things, so Murder Hornets were forgotten.

Make Your Own Luck

What can pimps and divorce lawyers teach children, about money and luck? This book tells the story of outdated wisdom and harsh truths.

Cockroach-baby smells really musky. Centipede baby was sewn from human skin. Squid-fish lives deep down in the sea. Flesh-eating ladybug is super scary. Bearded baby was born this hairy.

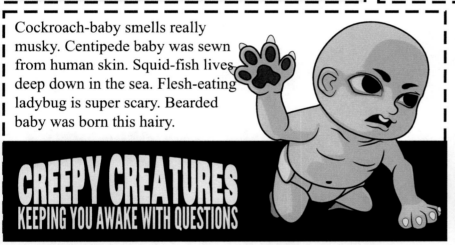

CREEPY CREATURES
KEEPING YOU AWAKE WITH QUESTIONS

SOFA KING

KLUKEE
The Plant Based Chicken

OURS BABY
The Only Child Your Step Mom Loves

Your stepmom wants one thing from your dear old dad. Viable sperm and an empty house. Pack your bags it's time to grow up.

MOMMY GOT A DUI

Your mom has secrets. She hides her drinking from you… Until now. Mommy can't drive you to school and you're going to have to learn the bus routes.

INSOMNIAC & FRIENDS
The Clowns That Put You To Sleep

Yeetyeet likes to watch you sleep. Pickles under your bed he creeps. Switchblade eats your favorite stuffies. Pedo lures you away with puppies. Shifty plans to collect your teeth. Twisty smells your hair while you sleep. Clammy lives inside his van. Hank once had to kill a man. Tooty smells your dirty socks. Busby laughs at electric shocks. Twinkles spends the night robbing graves. Fappy keeps a few human slaves.

MY RACIST GRAN

WHY DADDY HITS MOMMY

A Kids Guide To Understanding Alcoholism

DEAD BABIES
COLORING BOOKS

TRIGGERED
Kids Guide To Cancel Culture

Easily offended is the new trend. People act outraged. Be careful, you might lose your job. Even though nobody is responsible for the feelings of others.

OK BOOMER

Boomer always complains at the store. But it was on sale yesterday!! When yesterday's special isn't available anymore. You shouldn't be such a slut. Boomer gives unsolicited advice. This smart phone is dumber than dirt. Boomer always struggles with his device. Boomer demands your supervisor.

CANDIS NUTS
Come In The Morning Each Day

MELT IN YOUR MOUTH

CINNAMON

A horse forced into the sex trade.

Brad Gosse

DON'T BATHE WITH UNCLE JOE
Setting Boundaries With Adults

Uncle Joe lost his job. For misconduct in the workplace. He's coming to stay with us. You're going to have to learn to avoid his hands and more importantly. NEVER bathe with uncle Joe.

THIRST TRAPS
Why Moms Phone Keeps Blowing Up

DADDY'S A SIMP
Don't Expect Much Inheritance

HUMPTY DUMPTY
Discovers Workplace Misconduct

Made in the USA
Coppell, TX
08 December 2023

25579731R00019